Here We Go 'Round the Year

Do you know . . .

A library is a magic castle with many Word Windows in it?

What is a Word Window?

If you answered, "A book," you're right.

A book is a Word Window because the words, and the pictures that tell about the words, let you look and see many things. Books are your windows to the wide, wide world around you.

CHILDRENS PRESS
HARDCOVER EDITION
ISBN 0-516-05736-7

CHILDRENS PRESS
PAPERBACK EDITION
ISBN 0-516-45736-5

Library of Congress Cataloging in Publication Data

Moncure, Jane Belk.
  Here we go round the year.

  (Magic castle readers)
  Summary: Twelve little teddy bears describe
the weather and activities associated with each
month of the year.
  [1. Months—Fiction.   2. Teddy bears—Fiction]
I. Hohag, ill.   II. Title.   III. Series:
Moncure, Jane Belk.   Magic castle readers.
PZ7.M739He 1988   [E]   87-13257
ISBN 0-89565-402-4

Here We Go 'Round the Year

by Jane Belk Moncure
illustrated by Linda Hohag

Created by

Distributed by CHILDRENS PRESS®
Chicago, Illinois

The Library —
A Magic Castle

Come to the magic castle
When you are growing tall.
Rows upon rows of Word Windows
Line every single wall.
They reach up high,
As high as the sky,
And you want to open them all.
For every time you open one,
A new adventure has begun.

Amy opens a
Word Window.
Here's what she
reads.

Twelve little bears play, "Here
we go 'round the year."

"Come and play,"
say the bears.
"Here we go. . . ."

January . . .

brings lots of snow.

Hop on a sled.
Away we go.

February . . .

brings slippery ice.

Put on your skates.
The ice is nice.

March . . .

March

brings a windy sky . . .

just right for helping
kites to fly.

April . . .

brings showers our way.

We make mud pies on a rainy day.

May . . .

brings flowers and butterflies.

June...

brings picnics and sunny skies.

July . . .

brings a Fourth of July parade . . .

balloons, ice cream and lemonade.

August...

brings trips to the swimming pool.

September . . .

brings books, pencils and school.

October . . .

brings leaves and . . .

fun-times together.

November . . .

brings mittens . . .

24

and cold, frosty weather.

December . . .

brings sleigh rides,

surprises, and then . . .

a new year begins all over again.

Twelve little bears say, "Can you
read the months of the year?"

How many months are there around the year?

Can you find your birthday month?